THE STEWARDESS'S DIARY - PART FOUR

USA

S.M. PRATT

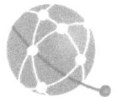

The Stewardess's Diary - Part Four: USA
Copyright © 2016 by S.M. Pratt

Last updated January 25th, 2020
Editing by Samantha Marie

ISBN: 978-0-9940630-7-6 (e-book)

ISBN: 978-1-988639-23-9 (paperback)

I'M CHARLIE, a veteran pilot for a major international airline that shall remain nameless for reasons you'll soon come to understand.

A year ago, while waiting for my flight to London in the airline's lounge at one of America's largest hubs, I discovered a special and highly personal journal among my belongings. How it happened, I'll never know, but the beautiful brown leather notebook nonetheless appeared in my briefcase at some point between the time I left my New York penthouse apartment and arrived at the airport lounge.

Perhaps it was a mix-up at security, or some devious stewardess with sly hand skills, but I've since become obsessed with the person who wrote that diary, her stories, and—to be blunt—her unconventional sex life.

My best friend—let's call him Bob—is one of my regular co-pilots. Bob advised me to forget about the journal and ignore my hunch to track down its rightful owner. After my initial reading of her hand-written accounts, the part of me who's loyal to the airline and wants the best for our passengers certainly needed to find that stewardess and expel her from our company—or whatever airline she's with. This woman is surely a threat to any crew with her irreverent disregard for our uniforms, her sexual behavior with passengers and airline employees, and the way she ignores regulations. She should clearly be punished for her conduct...

But after reading and re-reading each one of her journal entries, another, more animal part of me has grown fond of her complete lack of boundaries, her willingness to experiment, and her ravenous sexual appetite.

I've had my fair share of illicit affairs with female flight attendants and co-pilots, but none of them were interesting enough to be granted a second fuck by yours truly, let alone be courted or considered for a long-term relationship. But the woman who's filled so many pages with delicate calligraphy and salacious words deserves my full attention. She's certainly maintained it well past the time I closed the cover of her journal—again and again.

Imagining how her naiveté was gradually—and most willingly—robbed from her was simply... enthralling. She's been haunting my wet dreams.

Now, every time I see an unknown stewardess, I wonder if *she*'s the one.

After many conversations with Bob over the past months during our overseas flights, I've come to share some of her journal entries with him. He agrees that I need to locate her. If not for the airline's sake or to satisfy my personal curiosity, then for the mere reason that I could stop obsessing about her and resume paying attention to my actual job: piloting giant aircrafts and safely getting passengers from point A to point B.

The following short stories record my obsession toward her. There are ten in total. Each installment contains my mystery stewardess's original journal entries for a specific location, followed by my own experiences in trying to track her down. You'll discover what (and whom) I did in an effort to identify and locate my stewardess based on the clues she's left in her diary. You can read the episodes in any order, but they'll probably make more sense if you start from the beginning and follow along as I attempt to find her.

And, just to be clear, these stories should *not* land in the hands of any prude or underage person. Some are just romantic, sensual, or highly erotic, while others are immoral, perverse, and possibly even illegal in some parts of the world.

Ah, the things I'll do to this mystery stewardess when I finally encounter her in the flesh!

I'm hard just thinking about it...

Yours truly,

Capt. Charlie
Undisclosed Airline

PART ONE

THE STEWARDESS'S ENTRIES

AFTER HANDING the woman sitting in 5A her mini-bottle of Chardonnay and the chicken-breast sandwich she'd purchased, I peeked out of the porthole. Absolutely no clouds here. The same was expected for Los Angeles this weekend. In a few hours, I'd be seeing my friend Katrina, whom I haven't seen in ages... 13... 15 years already? I was looking forward to catching up with her over a couple of days.

I continued with the in-flight service, turning my attention to a distinct-looking blond man with shoulder-length wavy hair. He was quite handsome, save for his oddly crooked nose, but it added to his charm. I interrupted his chat with the young exotic woman sitting next to him. I couldn't tell her ethnicity, but she could have been the love child of an Asian-Brazilian couple. Long silky black hair draped over her shoulders, some of it falling over her large breasts. Her eyes were not almond-shaped to match her hair; they were round and light-colored. She reminded me of a National Geographic cover I'd seen years ago.

I smiled at them. "Sorry to interrupt, but what would you like to drink?" I asked the lady first, handing them both a paper napkin while waiting for her reply.

A shy smile preceded her words. Her green eyes met mine when she spoke. "Diet Pepsi, if you have it?"

"Diet Coke, okay?"

She nodded. I then turned my attention to the rugged man seated next to her.

"One second," he told me, his finger in the air while he turned to the woman. "Why don't I buy you a drink, to celebrate. After all, you're on your way to Hollywood." The woman's eyebrows slanted and so did her mouth. "Come on... One drink. On me. You may become a big star one day. I'd love to brag that I bought you a drink once."

She nodded, her cheeks registering a slight change toward pink.

The blond man turned toward me. "Let's make that two sparkling wines," he said while digging his wallet out.

"No problem. That will be eighteen dollars, sir."

I processed the payment and handed them the mini-bottles while reflecting on my friend Katrina, who, just like that young woman, had come to L.A. to make it. As far as I knew, Katrina still hadn't. The city was filled with young women like them, with big dreams and varying levels of acting talent.

I continued with the rest of the service, greeting people and serving them. Most were excited to be headed to sunny California: a family of seven was on their way to Disneyland; some were headed home for family reunions, and others were traveling for business purposes. Overall, the mood was definitely festive.

BY THE TIME I reached the back of economy, a bell chimed. I secured the trolley then walked toward the lit indicator. Blondie and Exotic-Girl were the ones who had requested my attention.

I arrived while he was finishing a sentence, "...And that's how I became a casting director."

"So, you hire actors?" she asked, her doe eyes fountains of innocence and hope.

"Of course," he replied before turning his attention to me.

"Hi, could you get us another two sparkling wines, please," he asked, a wide smile on his face, his hand now on the girl's knee.

"No problem, sir," I said. "I'll be right back."

Once in the galley, I grabbed the drinks then returned to Blondie's seat with my payment processing machine in hand. As I walked toward him, I noticed his head sticking out in the aisle. He was watching me come toward him, eyeing me up and down as though inspecting prey in a bar.

I tried to keep my skin from blushing, but I could feel heat rushing to my cheeks. *Is this shyness or arousal?* I didn't mind being ogled by a hottie, but I was working after all, and he was clearly hitting on Exotic-Girl sitting next to him. *What kind of man acts like this?* He pulled his head out of the aisle once I got within a couple of feet from him.

"Here you go, sir," I said, handing him the drinks.

We repeated the payment routine. I handed him the receipt along with the processed credit card, but he paused, his hands almost picking up the items but stopping short by an inch.

"This may sound a little strange, but my company is running auditions tomorrow, hoping to cast the role of a female flight attendant. I realize you've already got a job, but your work experience makes you the ideal candidate. The campaign is aimed at female flight attendants, just like you, who want to become pilots."

I frowned at him, confused. "You'd like me to participate in a movie?"

"No, no." He shook his head. "It's a publicity campaign. Short videos, pictures, posters, that sort of stuff."

"But I'm not based out of L.A.," I said, pushing the card and receipt toward him, hoping he'd grab them this time.

He did. "We're casting tomorrow and filming on Sunday. Very short-term gig. Possibly extra money if you get the part. Are you staying in town for the weekend?" he asked, his eyes now focusing on putting the credit card into its rightful slot in the black-leather wallet he was holding.

Is he serious? Maybe I'd get a chance to hook up with him... Then again, hard to compete with Exotic-Girl... but why not? Then I thought of Katrina. "Is this open to anyone?"

"Yeah, of course," he replied, now digging for something else in his wallet.

"I've got an acting friend who may be interested. Can she come, too?"

"The more the merrier," he said, pulling out a business card. "Tomorrow morning at 10 o'clock. This address," he said, pointing to the text that was printed on the front of the card.

"Thanks," I said, taking it from his hand.

"Hey! And me?" Exotic-Girl asked, apparently offended.

"Oh, of course you should come too! I was just about to mention it to you," I heard him say as I walked away, heading back toward the galley at the back of the plane.

I ALMOST DIDN'T RECOGNIZE Katrina when I saw her at the airport.

If it hadn't been for her jumping up and down and yelling out my name, I would have passed right by the silicone-breasted blonde woman in a mini-skirt and tank top.

"Katrina? What happened to you?"

Of course, I'd expected her to have changed. I'd seen some of her pictures on Facebook. I knew that she now flattened her naturally red and curly hair and that she'd dyed it blonde. But that body?

We hugged. She smelled of strawberries and cream. I pulled back, my hands holding hers, and had a good look at my friend.

"You look amazing!" I said while shaking my head in disbelief.

"Does that mean I looked awful before?" she asked. If I didn't know her, I would've worried about having offended her, but I knew it wasn't the case. She let go of my hands, her fake frown turned right-side up, and she finally explained. "Gotta put all the odds in my favor. Hollywood wants skinny blondes with big breasts. Here I am!" she exclaimed, hands on her hips, twisting her shoulders and posing à la Marilyn Monroe, her lips pursed in a sexy smooch.

"Wow. Good for you!"

"I gotta say that my tips at the bar have tripled since. Although I struggled to scrape the money I needed for the surgery, these babies have paid for themselves a couple of times over! But enough about that. Welcome to L.A. I'm so glad you'll be able to hang out with me. My boss gave me a couple of days off—don't ask what I had to do to get them—but I wanted to be around so we could catch up."

I wondered what she had to do to get time off. *Flash him her new breasts? Let him have a feel? Something else?*

"I thought we could relax and I could show you around town a bit. Are you hungry?" she asked.

I shrugged. "Sure, I could eat."

"Good, I've got a reservation at a raw-vegan bistro. You'll love it."

She started walking. I grabbed my wheeled bag and followed her toward the exit. I didn't know how she thought I would enjoy anything raw and vegan, considering we used to go out and share large plates of chicken wings, but I went along with her suggestion. If eating raw vegan food had helped shape her new body and rid her of a few pounds, it couldn't be bad.

After we crossed the automated doors and were greeted by a blended wave of warm air, exhaust, and smog, I announced my news to Katrina. "You won't believe it, but I've got us an audition for a publicity campaign tomorrow, if you're interested."

Her blue eyes went round. "Really? Awesome! What is it? And how did you..."

Cars driving by us made it hard for me to hear her. "Long story. I'll fill you in on the details on the way to the restaurant," I suggested as we crossed the road.

She nodded. "Awesome," she repeated.

THE WARMTH of the sun rays streaming in from the bare window woke me up. I opened my eyes. For a few seconds, I couldn't remember where I was, but then I saw Katrina lying next to me on the bed.

I rolled out of the pilled cotton sheets and placed my feet on the cracked tile floor on which the mattress rested. In front of me was a doorless, built-in closet where an assortment of plastic hangers were crammed, holding bright, colorful outfits. Piles of underwear, socks, and other clothes that weren't meant to be hung rested on the floor in a semi-organized fashion. Next to it, a large, unframed mirror leaned against the wall.

I heard water running in the room next door. *One of her two roommates taking a shower?*

"Hey," Katrina grunted in a raspy voice.

"Good morning," I said, turning to face her. "Did you sleep well?"

She nodded, her eyes blinking away her sleepiness. She cleared her throat then asked, "What time is it?"

I scanned the rest of her bedroom. No dresser or nightstand to support an alarm clock. I reached over to my purse, which I'd left against the wall next to my opened suitcase. I found my phone and looked at the screen. "7:30," I replied.

Katrina rubbed her face. "What time is that audition again?"

"Starts at 10 the man said."

As if someone had injected her with caffeine, Katrina jumped out of bed and rushed from the room. A second later, I heard banging on a door.

"Bunny! Hurry up and get out already. I've got an audition."

"You're not the only one. Wait your freaking turn, Kat!" a voice yelled over the running water.

Katrina came back and sat next to me on the bed, a defeated look on her face.

I tried to offer a comforting smile. "Not the best roommate relationship?"

"Nah," she said, raising her shoulders. "We're all trying to catch our big break. Jealousy gets the best of us at times. But it's okay."

She got back up and exhaled loudly and slowly, three times in a row. "I'll pick my clothing and do other things to get ready anyway."

I PUT on a pair of jean shorts and a white T-shirt after taking a very short shower—Bunny had graciously used up all the hot water.

I was blow-drying my hair when Katrina walked back in, her hair wrapped in a pink cotton turban and her body barely covered by a matching towel, the corners of which she held under her armpit in an effort to keep her enlarged breasts from bursting out of it. I saw her lips move, so I turned off the hair-dryer.

"Is this what you're wearing to the audition?" she asked, pointing at my outfit with her free hand.

I took a glance at what I was wearing. "I didn't bring much clothing. Mostly shorts and T-shirts...

and a bikini since I thought we might go to the beach."

"Believe me, from the hundreds of mostly unsuccessful auditions I've been to, you have to look sexier than that if you want to even stand a chance at getting the part. Why don't you pick something from my closet?" A smile grew on her face. "Now that I've got bigger boobs, my clothes will probably fit you."

DRESSED in a very short hot pink summer dress with spaghetti straps, I finally received Katrina's approval. She had donned a bright green tube dress that barely reached mid-thigh. My friend and I headed to the audition in the same Toyota she had owned since high school, many, many moons ago.

While driving and swerving her way through side roads and avoiding grid-locked streets, Katrina shared how her career was coming along—or not. She'd landed a few commercials and one-time appearances as a side-character in various TV shows, none of which I'd heard of. But her unrelenting enthusiasm and positivity were nothing short of impressive. *I'm happy she's got a part-time job to cover her living expenses.*

After a short detour caused by slightly inaccurate instructions provided by my phone's GPS app, we finally arrived at the address shown on the business card five minutes before the auditions were to start.

9:55 A.M.

A LARGE CARDBOARD sign stapled to a wooden post read "Capt. Dick Harding Flying School - Casting Auditions." The hand-written words were followed by an arrow. We headed in the direction indicated, then saw a few more smaller signs until we found ourselves on the third floor of a large office building.

We knew we'd reached our final destination when we walked into a sizable reception area where about fifty women, most of whom were dressed provocatively, sat on black plastic chairs filling out forms. *Guess Katrina was right about my outfit.* A strong aroma of mixed perfumes filled the air. Light background music sounded from a speaker in the corner next to us. I glanced around the room and recognized Exotic-Girl from the plane. She wore a mini-skirt and tank top. Before I could walk over to say, "Hi," a young woman in jeans and a Capt. Dick Harding Flying School T-shirt greeted us and handed each of us our own stack of forms and a pen. "Please take a seat and fill these out," she said.

We sat together near the back of the room and started filling out the forms. At first, it was nothing out of the ordinary: name, date of birth, social security number, previous acting experience, etc. But then, a few fields appeared odd to me.

"Why are they asking for my ethnicity, bra size, weight, and height?" I asked Katrina.

She shrugged. "That's common. Could be because the part calls for a particular body type, or maybe their outfits need to be tailored, so they're just saving themselves some back and forth, collecting the data they need now."

Makes sense, I guess.

Once we'd filled out all required information, we handed our paperwork to the same woman. She informed us that we could use one of the lockers to store our purses and other valuables if we so desired. The idea of lugging it all morning didn't really appeal to me, so I did and Katrina did the same. Then, we sat down to wait, our locker keys attached to our wrists.

I tried to make eye contact with Exotic-Girl, but sensed that she was avoiding my glance. I didn't want to bother her, so I gave up on the idea. I turned my attention to the other women in the room: some of them were repeating some tongue twisters, others were nonchalantly scooping their hands in their tops to adjust their breasts in their outfits, a couple of very young girls were fixing their make-up. I looked at Katrina: she was biting her nails.

"It'll be fine," I said, winking and tapping her on the knee.

"Do you know how much the part pays?" she asked me.

I shook my head. "No idea."

And just then, the lady we'd handed our forms to called for everyone's attention. "I'm going to read a list of names. If you hear yours, please proceed through the door behind me. If not, we thank you for your time and you're free to go home."

"Already?" I asked, surprised.

Katrina lifted her shoulders. "They're probably

looking for a specific age group or ethnicity," she whispered to me.

The woman started listing names and Katrina grabbed my hand, squeezing it as though it would increase our odds.

HAVING SUCCESSFULLY MADE it past their pre-selection filter, Katrina and I joined the other lucky women behind the door, which opened onto a long and bare hallway painted light gray.

At the end of the corridor, just before another door, sat a short & skinny bald man who also wore a white Capt. Dick Harding Flying School T-shirt. He turned out to be responsible for the second part of the selection process. With a nod or a shake of the head, he picked which of us could go past the next door.

The woman in front of Katrina and me, a tall, strong and athletic brunette with a *don't-mess-with-me* attitude was turned away. Her traits immediately morphed into the same saddened expression that had colored the faces of the women who had been eliminated just a few minutes ago.

Thankfully, Katrina and I got the nod and proceeded into what appeared to be a large change room.

Hot pink flight attendant skirts as well as white short-sleeved shirts filled two large racks, and rows of black high-heeled shoes were neatly lined below them.

Katrina high-fived me. "We're doing great," she whispered in my ear.

No wonder it's hard to make it as an actress. We haven't even said a word yet! I counted the women in the room. We'd already dropped from the approximate fifty that had shown up to twenty-five. Exotic-Girl had also made it.

Another woman dressed in the flying school's T-shirt measured us around the breast, waist, and ass. She then yelled out our measurements to a young, effeminate man standing by the rack of clothes who, a minute later, would hand us the exact sizes we'd each need. We were ordered to change into the outfits.

About a dozen staff members, men and women, all in the same uniforms, were roaming the room, notepads in hand and talking to each other. I turned to Katrina, unsure about the procedure to follow. "Are there change rooms?"

"Probably not," she said after glimpsing the room.

The increased confidence and improved self-image I'd gained over the past few months proved worthwhile. Not that long ago, I would've been very, very uncomfortable getting undressed in front of that many men and women. But I was much more comfortable with my body now; the idea of changing in front of people even made a slight thrill go up my spine.

I started undoing the first of the many delicate buttons on the sexy summer dress I'd borrowed from Katrina while glancing around the room. Katrina pulled down her green dress in one swift motion before stepping out of it. Her large, perky silicone implants and white panties were soon covered by the white cotton shirt. About half-way done with my buttons, I met the glance of another woman for a second, but she kept scanning the room before shaking her head. She then walked out the way we'd come in.

The last of my tiny buttons undone—there must have been about twenty-five of those—I finally slipped out of my dress and put on the uniform I'd been handed. The pink polyester skirt ended three inches above my knees. The waist and hips fitted nicely enough. The white shirt, however, was a bit tight. The two chest-height buttons threatened to pop and fly across the room. I looked at Exotic-Girl, who stood a few feet away from me. Her breasts also pushed the confines of her shirt; the embroidered details of her red bra pushed through the fabric enough for a blind person to read their Braille-like contours.

"Okay, ladies. Once you're dressed, go find a pair of shoes that fits, then stand in line, ready for inspection," a man said.

The voice sounded familiar. I turned to see who it was, and I recognized the blond man from the plane.

"That's the casting director who told me about this," I whispered to Katrina.

She leaned toward me. "He's cute. Tall. Blond. Totally your type!"

He walked slowly in front of us, reminding me of a military official inspecting troops in a movie, except that his nod or shake meant whether or not we'd proceed to the next step in the audition.

"Hey, you made it," he said when he reached

me in the line.

I smiled. "And I brought my friend Katrina," I said, pointing to her standing next to me.

"Katrina," he said, eyeing her up and down. "Nice."

Katrina and I both got the nod, and he continued his inspection of the other women past us. I overheard him greet Exotic-Girl. She was standing a few women down the line from us, giggling and grinning at the casting director. *Oh dear. That's the look of an infatuated young girl. She probably slept with him last night... Good for her. And it doesn't necessarily mean my odds are nil. It's not as though I'd want him for the rest of my life. I just want to experience him a little... And it's not as though I could have called him up yesterday anyway. What kind of a friend shows up, then says she's got other plans and heads out to meet a man instead of hanging out with the friend who's invited her?*

A few minutes later, the third round of the selection process was over and our count had officially dropped to twenty, including Katrina, Exotic-Girl and me.

The unsuccessful candidates were stripping out of their uniforms and donning their own clothes when the casting director told us to gather up around him.

11:00 A.M.

"GOOD MORNING, LADIES," the director started. "First of all, thank you for coming to this audition and for looking so lovely. We're casting the role of a flight attendant this morning. It's for a print and video advertising campaign targeting female flight attendants who want to become pilots. Capt. Dick Harding Flying School is no regular aviation program. They're passionate about what they do. They hand-pick those who join their ranks. Only select women that meet very stringent entry criteria and who truly feel destined to become pilots are invited to join their school. Your performance here today will have to reflect that aching passion in your heart," he said, tapping on his chest. "You'll have to perform; you'll have to show us that you'd do a-ny-thing to join their ranks. A-ny-thing," he repeated, accentuating the syllables once more. "Are you ready to do that today?" he asked our group, his voice that of a coach trying to psych his football team up for a big game.

A few heads nodded, including mine.

The casting director frowned and shook his head. "Are you ready to act passionately and do anything for this part?" he repeated, this time yelling.

A resounding, "Yes," echoed from my mouth and that of the other women around me.

"Good," he said, grinning and nodding. "Now, please line up next to each other behind the tracks here." He pointed to an area of the floor near us. "Stand about two feet away from each other."

Once we were positioned in our appropriate spots, the casting director continued with his speech. "Our artistic vision for this campaign is very emotional and avant-garde. To visually represent your inner desire to become a pilot, we will tattoo wings on your heart, where the real pilot wings that you want will hopefully be pinned one day. So, please undo your shirt, and one of our assistants will apply a temporary tattoo above your left breast," he said before turning around to face the people who were standing behind him. He snapped his fingers.

A small group of men and women headed our way, each with a small pail, a rag, and a few other things in hand. A cameraman moved and started recording, a red light blinking from his gear.

We're being filmed now?

The short bald man who'd previously manned the hallway door stood in front of me, waiting for me to undress so he could apply the wing tattoo. I undid five buttons and opened my shirt to clear my left breast, then moved my bra strap out of the way.

"I gotta clean the skin first," he said before unwrapping an alcohol wipe from its envelope.

I nodded.

He unfolded a small rectangular tissue then brought it to the top of my breast to wipe the area. A faint smell of lemon reached my nose. He then placed the wet, used tissue in his short pocket. A second later, he grabbed the temporary tattoo, peeled off the plastic sheet covering the image, and then placed the wings against my skin, just above my breast. While he held the tattoo on me with one hand, he dipped the other into a small bucket and then pressed the cold wet rag on the tattoo area, patting the paper lining. A few drips dropped into my white bra.

"I gotta keep the paper wet for about thirty seconds," he said, patting some more, then soaking the rag into the pail. Once again, he brought it back to my chest and repeated the patting. I looked at his balding head, a few drips of sweat beaded on his forehead and a light musky smell mixed with a Cheetos aroma emanated from him. More cold water dripped into my bra. Every few seconds, just when the rag would start getting a little warmer— less freezing would be more accurate—the man would dip it into his pail again. *Really? Again? Does tattoo application require frigid water?*

I turned to look at Katrina, standing a couple of feet from me, receiving a similar treatment from a young woman. We exchanged smiles. Then the cold rag moved away from the tattoo area.

What the heck?

I looked down at my left breast. The man was now pressing his wet cold rag directly onto the center of my breast, making that part of my white bra transparent and forcing my nipple to harden even more. The bald man's eyes were glued on my breast. He had a slanted grin on his face, exposing a few yellow teeth. A tented bulge formed in his loose shorts. Although the thought of slapping the man crossed my mind, I didn't. Why risk ruining Katrina's odds... or mine? *The poor man isn't the handsomest. It may have been a while since he last saw a nipple that wasn't on his computer screen...*

"How are those tattoos coming along?" the casting director asked loudly in the background.

The man in front of me returned his wet rag up to the tattoo area.

"I'm gonna peel it off now," he said after licking his lips and bringing his eyes up by a few inches. He tugged on one edge of the paper and removed it, revealing a large set of beautiful golden pilot wings. "And now I have to keep the area wet for a little while, to make sure it won't peel off," he said before re-dipping the rag into the icy water pail.

Once again, his rag started in the tattoo area, but explored further south than it had to. His hand then went for an unrequested, full-hand squeeze of my breast.

"Hey!" I discreetly uttered. *What's going on in this guy's mind?*

He shrugged, then winked at me and told me I could button up my shirt again. He grabbed his things then walked away, still erect in his shorts.

I shook my head and brought my bra strap up

then buttoned my blouse while glancing around me at the other women.

Am I the only one who got the creepy perverted treatment?

Hard to tell, but most had gotten their tattoo and were standing still, many braless with perky nipples poking through their tight white shirts. Very few wore bras.

Surely this isn't normal for an audition, right?

A couple of girls still had an assistant standing in front of them, but they appeared to be nearly done.

Dead center in front of our line of hopeful candidates, the casting director sat in a movie-director chair, a large monitor at his feet. The man I'd seen earlier, the one walking with a camera on his shoulder, had now relocated his gear to the dolly at one end of the rails.

A few minutes later, his camera anchored to the dolly, the cameraman started filming the first woman on the far right, about a dozen feet away from me.

"Dave, zoom in," the casting director ordered.

The cameraman moved his hand on his apparatus.

"No, I can't see the tattoo," the casting director started, shaking his head. He got up. "Ladies," he continued, now in a louder voice, "unbutton your shirts some more, so the camera can capture your new tattoo."

I obeyed, undoing two buttons and pulling the fabric away toward my shoulder. Women around me did the same.

"No, this won't do," the director said, his eyes still glued on the monitor in front of him. "I still can't see the full tattoo. Take off your shirts," he ordered.

I turned to Katrina. "This is normal?" I asked her while undoing the rest of my shirt's buttons.

She raised her shoulders and nodded.

Strange.

Katrina's enlarged breasts were fully exposed, her small nipples pointing straight forward. I looked around the room and less than half of us in hot-pink skirts and high heels had bras on.

Were women once again going through a revolution of sorts? Did I miss a social media campaign about women giving up wearing bras for one reason or another?

"Much better," the casting director said, still looking at the monitor in front of him. The cameraman crept his way along the tracks. About three women later, the casting director spoke again. "No, no, no." He shook his head. "Those with bra straps, we can't see the full tattoo. Take your bras off."

A couple of women walked out, this last request probably proving to be too much.

Katrina looked at me, and we both shrugged.

She leaned toward me and whispered, "Exposed breasts aren't a big deal. Common in auditions, really. And it's for the director's creative vision."

I obeyed, undoing the back clasp, then tossing my white bra at my feet, along with the shirt I'd removed earlier. I saw the man who had put on my tattoo standing a few feet behind the director. He was staring at me, another creepy grin on his face, a hand in his pocket. The fabric of his shorts may have been covering his erect dick, but it didn't hide the fact that he was touching himself right now. *Does his pocket have a big hole in it, allowing his hand to stroke his cock like that?*

I felt a shiver go up my spine, not from the bald, creepy man touching himself but from the cold breeze that had suddenly started blowing on us. I rubbed my goose-bump-covered arms in an effort to warm up.

"Stand tall, ladies," the casting director said, still looking at the monitor in front of him. "Bring those shoulders back. Imagine you're already a pilot. Your dream's come true! Show us how delighted you are to have gotten those pilot wings. Place your hands on your hips. Look up. Be proud!"

The cameraman kept moving slowly on the tracks in front of us.

"Now, that's what I'm talking about! Good work, ladies. Keep that position," the casting director said, now taking his eyes off of the monitor to look at us directly.

He stood up and, with two fingers, motioned for a Latino man with a Canon hung around his neck to come toward him.

"These tattoos are looking good, ladies. Pedro and I will now take your mug-shot to see how photogenic you are," the director said.

While the cameraman continued filming us from the dolly rig—he was about three-quarters done now—the casting director and Pedro headed to the first woman standing on the far right.

They spent a couple minutes in front of her. Being out of the cameraman's vision field, I turned my attention to what the cute director was doing. He was looking at the man's camera screen after the shots were taken, then he addressed the brunette in front of him. "Thank you for coming out. You're lovely, but it won't work for our campaign." The woman let out a loud sigh, then bent down to grab her bra and shirt from the floor in front of her. "Please return the uniform on your way out," he said with a large smile as she stormed away.

What was the deciding factor?

I turned to Katrina and kept silent. She too had seen that woman walk away. She raised her shoulders.

Once the photographer and casting director arrived in front of me. I returned to the pose, standing proud, pushing my breasts out, hands on my hips, looking at the camera. At first, the photographer was taking a picture of my face, then it was obvious most of his 'mug-shots' were in fact 'jug-shots.' The Latino man wasn't just taking a picture of the tattoo. He was aiming his Canon way too low for that, but the blonde lesbians I'd met in Mexico did tell me my breasts were awesome. Who better than them to know? *Let them have great shots of my beautiful girls.* I pushed my shoulders back even more, making eye contact with the blond hottie. He quietly nodded, a spark appearing in his eyes before winking at me. A sense of pride entered my mind. *No... Not pride. Probably lust.*

A minute later, the two men moved to Katrina.

She was looking up, her tits bulging forward. I admired her enhanced breasts for a moment. I was glad she'd gotten a good boob job. With all of the horror stories I'd seen on TV with one nipple pointing left and the other down, or weird bumps deforming the natural drop-shaped breasts... The photographer took several shots—of her face but mostly her breasts—then the two men moved on to the next woman.

"Yeah!" she quietly said to me, exposing all of her whitened teeth in a smile and jumping up and down, her silicone twins bouncing in an unnatural rhythm. "We both still stand a chance!"

I smiled.

While I was a little baffled that my friend hadn't realized these men were just taking advantage of us —creative vision my ass—I decided there was no real harm being done.

I might as well enjoy myself in the process. Who knows, maybe this could turn into a date or one-night stand with the cute blond director?

The thought of seeing him naked moistened my panties.

PEDRO AND DAVE now done with the latest phase of the auditioning process, the remaining twelve of us—including Exotic-Girl, Katrina, and me—were once again ordered to gather around.

"Okay, ladies. You're doing fantastic," the casting director said, his large encouraging smile still decorating his rugged, handsome face. His crooked nose was really growing on me. "All of you still stand a very good chance at being hired for this publicity campaign. But we need to see your walking stroll so that we know if you can really portray the way a proud captain would walk to the departure gate, ready to pilot a large Boeing 747 to some exciting destination. Of course, the flight attendant's uniforms won't do for that. You'll have to change into a captain's jacket."

He snapped his fingers and the effeminate man rolled a new rack of clothing toward us. This time, it was filled with navy-blue uniforms.

The jackets were one-sized: men's small. We each grabbed one from the rack, then I stepped away from the crowd to strip and don the new outfit. Katrina joined me a few seconds later.

"I'm so excited," she whispered as she unzipped her skirt. "I rarely make it this far! There's only twelve of us. We stand a really good chance," she said, her eyes exploding with hope.

I smiled at her, putting on the pilot's jacket. *I can't crush her hopes. But maybe I'm just wrong. Who am I to tell, really... It could be a legit audition?*

"No pink skirts," the casting director yelled out.

The rack in front of us was now empty. No skirts therefore meant no bottoms at all.

"Keep those bras off as well," the director yelled out. Exotic-Girl dropped down the red lacy bra she'd picked up from the floor in front of her. "Nothing wrong with your lacy undergarments, ladies. But we don't want the color of them distracting us from the professional look of the uniform. You don't want to lower your odds at being selected for this role, right?"

I buttoned the double-breasted jacket and pulled on the front, trying to make it drape as best as possible on me, but it was all in vain. The jacket ended a couple of inches below my white panties. The V-opening of the flaps showed a good forty percent of my cleavage, but it wasn't supported by my underwire bra. *I can't say that my girls look as sexy now as they do when supported...*

"Okay, ladies," the casting director continued once all of us had donned the new uniform. "This next phase is really simple. All you have to do is walk in front of the green screen, rolling a carry-on bag behind you. Simple, right? But remember to smile and look proud. Any questions?" he asked.

I glanced around. The other women were shaking their heads, some trying to pull down the jacket a bit more, some trying to close the deep opening in the front to cover their breasts. The one-sized jacket appeared particularly short on one red-headed woman with a long torso; her blue boy-cut panties were half visible below it. One young and extremely large-breasted woman couldn't even cover her dark brown nipples with the lapels of her jacket.

Katrina and I stood sixth and seventh in line, just behind Exotic-Girl. The director sat a few feet away from the line of women waiting for their turn. The effeminate man brought a pilot's hat and a black wheeled suitcase to the first woman in line.

She strolled in front of the director a couple of times, following his orders, then passed the props to the next woman, who was eliminated right away. So was the one in front of Exotic-Girl. No reasons were voiced aloud, but the two women certainly didn't have the slenderest legs among our group.

On Exotic-Girl's first attempt at strolling past the screen, she was stopped by the director.

"No. Go back and try again," he said, pointing her back to our side of the screen. "Chin up, smile, look proud, but walk a little slower, please."

She repeated her stroll. "Good, but do it again, this time, running toward the gate as if you're urgently making your way to save a passenger's life."

I frowned at the unlikely suggestion, then took a few steps back to peek at the monitor sitting in front of the director to get an idea of what he was focusing his attention on. Exotic-Girl began her stroll again, the camera zoomed to frame her from neck to mid-thigh. We couldn't even see her face.

Her bouncing tits and the barely covered red panties were the stars here.

"Great," the casting director said. "Pass the hat and luggage to the next woman."

It was now Katrina's turn. I returned to her just as she received the luggage prop. "Go for it, Kat. Be confident and proud," I whispered in her ear before squeezing her shoulder.

Katrina walked away toward the fake airport gate, black suitcase in tow, her blonde hair tucked under the captain's hat. She repeated the walk a couple of times, then the director announced it was my turn.

After a few strolls at varying speeds, I joined Katrina with the rest of the women who had passed the latest audition stage. To congratulate me, my friend high-fived me, which didn't go unnoticed by the director.

"Hey, girls. Do that again, but can you jump up in the air this time?"

Katrina and I looked at each other and nodded. I took a few steps back and we ran toward each other. We both jumped before our hands met in mid-air. I turned to look at the director and noticed a cameraman aiming his camera our way.

"That's wonderful, ladies," the director said.

"Very representative of how it'd feel to graduate from the aviation school."

He called out louder this time, getting the attention of all of the women still auditioning.

"Ladies, you saw what these two just did? Pair up, then you'll run up to each other, jump up in the air, and high five each other, large smiles on your face. You've graduated. All of your hard, hard work has paid off."

Running up in high heels and then jumping up to high-five another person turned out to be quite a difficult task to do for many of us, but the cameraman and director were patient. After Katrina and I had redone the feat once more, I discreetly repositioned myself behind the cameraman, just to see what he was recording. As I suspected, he was zooming in on the edges of our jackets. Jumping with an arm raised was making them lift up, exposing our panties, and in this particular case, one woman's shaved pussy, since she didn't have any underwear on. Just the captain's jacket.

Katrina was standing a few feet from me, beaming and looking at the other contestants, apparently still clueless as to what was really going on. I walked over to her to chat while the last pair of women got ready for their camera time.

"So, this... audition," I started whispering in her ear. "Does it follow a similar process to what you've been through before?"

She raised her shoulders and eyebrows. "So far, most of it seems quite common. I've had to do similar things in previous interviews. Not always in group settings, though. Directors always have a creative vision, and they must ensure the actors they hire will properly portray their vision. Makes sense, no?"

I nodded.

Why shatter my friend's hopes? What's the harm in letting her think she still stands a chance at being hired? She obviously doesn't mind being objectified... It could even boost her self-confidence for future auditions? After all, she and I are now part of the top ten finalists for this "advertising gig" ...if we can call it that.

1:45 P.M.

AFTER A BRIEF LUNCH BREAK—THEY'D provided their crew and us, the ten remaining candidates, with an assortment of pastries, mini-sandwiches, raw veggies, and dips—we were ordered to change back into our flight attendant's pink uniforms and gather around the casting director yet again.

"Hope you enjoyed your free meal. Now, we'll record a demo lesson. Please take a seat in the classroom next door." He motioned for us to head toward the back of the lunch room.

The classroom setting was reminiscent of one of those mini university auditoriums, as I'd seen them in movies, with rows of chairs, each higher than the other. A muscular man stood behind a large wooden stand that occupied the middle of the floor in front of an immaculate white board that read *AVIATION 101* in bold black letters. The tanned, crew-cut, brown-haired man wore a tight white, short-sleeved shirt that almost ripped on his carved biceps. Pilot wings were pinned above his left breast pocket.

We each took a seat.

"He's cute," Katrina whispered in my ear as the director walked to chat with the instructor. "I wouldn't mind getting private lessons from him!"

I smiled in agreement. He was definitely handsome, although a little too young for me.

The cameraman stood with his gear on his shoulder; he was focusing on the instructor. Upon hearing the director's cue, the hot instructor smiled, welcomed us, then started his lesson about the four forces acting on planes: lift, weight, thrust, and drag. The instructor read long-winded definitions from a teleprompter in front of him.

"...When the thrust becomes greater than the drag, the plane accelerates forward, which is best explained by Newton's Second Law of Motion..."

I was trying to pay attention to his lesson, but his physique was more interesting than his words. I could only imagine how defined his abdominals had to be. *Does he have a six- or an eight-pack? He probably spends the rest of his waking hours lifting weights at the gym... or doing whatever woman throws herself at him.*

That had to happen quite often for such a stud. And he even sounded intelligent while reading those lines. I was unsure if he was as smart as he sounded, but I gave him the benefit of the doubt. My eyes veered toward the blond director, now sitting in the front row. He was more my type. Probably very intelligent, although he was clearly a manipulative man who excelled at fooling women and getting them naked in front of a camera... not the most respectful of men... but just looking at him made me tingle and got me wet where it mattered. *Unsure why exactly. Maybe it's his air of power... or something about his crooked nose... Is it the result of some well-deserved punch in the face by one of his lovers' husbands?*

"...Newton's Laws and Bernoulli's Principle explain how lift is generated..." the instructor continued. I returned my focus to him. His lips moved, but I didn't want to pay attention to his words.

Then, as if he'd realized how much of a bore he was, he grabbed a pile of papers from the stand in front of him and waved them in the air.

"I hope you've been listening because it's now time for a pop quiz!" he said, finally moving from behind the lectern, where he'd remained since the beginning of his lecture, which had started about ten minutes ago.

What I saw surprised me. I had expected him to wear the traditional navy-blue or black pants that pilots normally wore, but instead, he had on tight white shorts, probably made of a mix of Spandex, rayon, or similar. His mini shorts clung to his every curve and groove, leaving nothing to the imagination. His shirt was tucked in, a silver buckle differentiating where the shirt ended and where the shorts began, but something else hadn't quite been tucked all the way in: his flaccid penis was running down his right thigh, and its surprising length—even at rest—meant that its tip was protruding, as if to say hello.

Quiet giggles and whispers echoed around me. It appeared we were all staring at the same part of his beautiful anatomy, but the instructor managed to keep his concentration and walked toward us to hand out quizzes, along with pencils.

"What the...?" Katrina asked as she poked me in the ribs.

"Still think this is a regular audition?" I asked her in a whisper.

She rolled her eyes before shaking her head. "...But he's so hot!"

Hot (and well-hung) actors are probably a requirement if the director wants his porn movies to be popular.

"Cut!" the director called out.

A tall Asian woman used the director's word as her cue to stand up and leave. "I'm out," she said before exiting the room. The brunette sitting next to her hesitated for a few seconds, then got up and followed her out.

I looked at Katrina, wondering if she was still interested. She raised her shoulders. "Some famous actresses had their break in porn," she whispered. "Are you still in? I'd understand if you wanted out."

"Why not," I said just as the hot guy handed me a piece of paper, his eyes glued on Katrina next to me. Katrina's pop quiz was delivered with a smile and a wink, then the hot instructor continued handing his sheets to the remaining women. "I'm curious to see how far they'll go... And so far, the experience has been... entertaining to say the least," I whispered to Katrina.

"Awesome. And maybe one of us will get the part... And maybe I can get this hot guy's phone number." Katrina's eyes were now focused on the instructor's firm glutes as he headed back to his stand.

While I was pretty sure there wasn't going to be a *part* other than what we were currently doing for free (or, to be more accurate, in exchange for a free lunch), I had no doubt she'd be able to get that man's number.

"Okay, ladies," the director, who had moved and now stood in front of the podium, called out. "You've each received a sheet of paper. On it are script lines, questions for you to ask the instructor. Take a few minutes now to familiarize yourself with your question and be ready to ask it aloud without reading from the paper. Remember, we're looking for passionate students! We'll record your performance to see how you come across on video."

I looked at mine:

I'm a woman who dreams to become a pilot.
Can I do it in such a men's world?

It wasn't going to be too hard to memorize. I concentrated on my lines and mentally repeated them for a few minutes until I no longer needed my piece of paper.

The casting director walked around the classroom while we were preparing. Some women were rehearsing aloud, and he was giving them feedback if and when asked.

No point in practicing aloud. I'll just wait my turn and do it live.

A few more minutes went by, then the classroom got quiet again. The eight of us that remained were ready for this next part. My cute crooked-nosed crush got up and stood next to the instructor before addressing us again.

"So, there's a number in the top-right corner of your sheet. We'll use this number to determine the order. Whoever has number one can come down here and stand next to the instructor."

Exotic-Girl stood up and, in her four-inch heels, slowly walked down the steps that separated her from the two handsome men. The director had returned to his seat by the time she arrived next to the instructor. She fluffed her ebony hair over her shoulders, straightened her back, pushing her breasts out in the process, then smacked her bright red luscious lips.

"Ready?" the director asked her.

"Yes," she replied, all smiles.

"Are you ready, Nick?" the director asked the instructor.

He inhaled deeply, then nodded.

The director turned his attention to Exotic-Girl again. "Okay, stand next to him, both of you facing the camera, and touch him on the forearm when you ask your question. Clear?"

Exotic-Girl nodded.

"And... Action!"

She flicked her eyelashes at the instructor, then her delicate hand grabbed his tanned, muscular forearm.

"But learning to be a pilot... it's hard, right?" she asked with puppy eyes.

He wrapped his arm around her waist as he replied, his eyes locked on her breasts, which heaved noticeably as she breathed. Maybe the wave-like motion of her chest was caused by the stress of the audition. Or it could have been a natural reflex based on her innate feminine sex appeal or the pheromone effect of standing next to a hottie in tight white shorts.

"A lot of things are hard here," he said before pausing, as though concentrating on something. His other hand went to the side of his own waist, in a Mr.-Clean-esque pose. My own eyes diverted to what was happening in his shorts: his dick elongated and widened in girth. A few glorious inches were now fully exposed out of his shorts, the fabric barely able to keep it from going up. I realized my jaw had dropped a second later, just as he pulled on the waist of his shorts and the fabric ripped, letting his full manhood bounce up, exposing his clean-shaven genitals.

The cameraman was recording all of it: the half-naked man ready for action, Exotic-Girl's surprised expression, the audience's whispers and utters, as well as three of the remaining candidates leaving the group, clearly offended.

"Cut!" the director said. "Great job. On to number two. Please come down."

A bleached-blonde girl who couldn't be older than eighteen or nineteen walked down and stood next to the erect instructor. She blushed, then turned and focused her attention on the director.

"Ready?" the director asked both parties.

She nodded and so did he.

"And... Action!"

She turned to look at the instructor, her eyes locked with his. "How's Capt. Dick Harding Flying School different from the other aviation schools in town?" she asked.

He turned to the cameraman. "We stand behind our students, all the way," he said before taking a couple of steps to reposition himself behind the tall blonde woman, his hands grabbing her by the hips. Her innocent eyes suddenly widened and her already blushing cheeks somehow cranked up to crimson; his erect dick had clearly poked her somewhere. From where I sat, I couldn't quite tell if any direct skin contact had occurred, but the cameraman was moving around to record the best angle.

"Cut, great job. Great reaction," the director said to the young girl. "It's good when actors express their emotions like that. You can go back to your seat." He turned to face the rest of us. "Who's number three?"

Nobody moved, except to look around.

The director raised his shoulders. "She must have left already. Better odds for those who remain! Number four?"

Katrina stood up and squeezed behind me on the way to the aisle.

"You go, girl," I whispered to her as she walked by. I didn't know what her question was going to be, but I was excited. I was about to experience the first real acting part of the audition for my childhood friend.

Katrina stood next to the hot instructor, who whispered something in her ear. She pulled back to make eye contact with him and nodded, a large grin on her face.

Did he ask her out on a date? When she started unbuttoning her shirt, I realized his question had to have been different. The last button undone, she removed her shirt and tossed it on the ground. Her exposed tits had the effect of scaring away one more candidate, who left quietly through the back door. *The erect dick hadn't clued her in?* Only four of us remained.

The director addressed Katrina. "You stand over there and look my way. For number four, you'll ask me your question, and the instructor will be behind you, off camera, until he replies. Are you ready?"

They both positioned themselves according to the director's instructions, then the recording began.

"What can I expect from Capt. Dick Harding Flying School?" Katrina asked.

"Cut!"

Katrina sent the scared glance of a hunted

bunny my way. *What? What did she do wrong? Her question sounded natural.* The director explained himself immediately.

"It'd be better if you raised your hand to ask your question. You did well, just raise your hand first, then repeat the question the way you did it a second ago. It was great."

A sigh of relief came out of both her mouth and mine. I turned my attention to the monitor at the director's feet. It showed the cameraman's live output. Katrina's entire body was framed in the shot, alone. The instructor was standing just out of view. When the director called "Action!" she raised her hand, making one of her augmented breasts go higher than the other, then she repeated her question. "What can I expect from the Capt. Dick Harding Flying School?"

She lowered her arm and a second passed. Still hard, Hot-Instructor walked into the shot. He stood behind her, cupped Katrina's breasts and answered, looking directly at the cameraman. "We offer one-on-one support. With us, you'll be in good hands." He gave her breasts a gentle squeeze.

The camera zoomed in on the both of them: her breasts and his hands now the only visible body parts.

"Cut! Good work, both of you."

Katrina smiled and bent down to grab her shirt. Hot-Instructor slapped her on the ass and she jumped back up. "Hey!"

"Couldn't resist," he said.

She smiled at him, then whispered something in his ear as she buttoned up her shirt. He nodded, then she walked back up the steps and returned to her seat, squeezing my shoulder when she passed behind me.

"Got a date with him tonight!" she said.

I smiled at her. *At least one good thing will come out of this for Katrina!*

"Okay," the director said after standing up and turning to face us. He scanned the room, as though counting how many gullible want-to-be-actresses were still present. "Looks like we have one left to go. Number five or whatever your number is."

I got up and walked down to center stage, next to Hot-Instructor. I wondered what sexual innuendo they had planned for my particular question. I looked at the instructor's erect member and felt my pussy twitch. I turned my attention to the other hottie, my crooked-nose director, to await his instructions.

"What question do you have?" he asked.

"Seven," I said.

He flipped through the flash cards he held and read some hand-written notes. He looked back up at me, a large grin on this face and a sparkle in his eye. "Perfect. Looking forward to this. Same as your friend. Address the camera, and the instructor will come in later."

I nodded.

"Ready? And... Action!"

I looked directly at the camera and asked my question: "I'm a woman who dreams to become a pilot—"

"Cut!"

"No, if you really dream to be a pilot, you need to have that desperate desire in your eyes. I need more passion. Show me you're CRAVING it. Imagine that huge airplane in the air. You want to be in control, you want to be the one in charge. You want to be a pilot!"

He got up and walked toward me. His hands pushed my shoulders back, and I pushed my breasts forward. *More confidence, more pride.* As I did so, however, my top button gave up—the tightness of the shirt proved to be too much for the poor piece of thread that had held the button in place for so long already.

"Ah!" the director said as the button hit him on the chest. "Call that a sign. Let's unbutton your shirt and expose your tattoo. That will help convey your inner drive to become a pilot."

His fingers unbuttoned my shirt, his eyes locked onto mine, his smile crooked. Electric currents flooded the small space between us. I wanted him and he knew it. The last button undone, he peeled off my shirt, his fingers brushing against my arms and FedExing a thrill all the way down to my pussy.

He took a step back and eyed me from head to toe. "Great. Now keep those shoulders back and repeat your question. Move your feet shoulder-width apart, you'll look more confident. Do it again... with passion this time!"

I inhaled deeply and spread my legs as he said, although that wasn't a natural pose. Who stands with their feet shoulder apart in a mini-skirt? I shook the idea out of my head, rolled my shoulders back, then inhaled deeply again before staring at the camera.

"I'm a woman who dreams to become a pilot. Can I do it in such a men's world?"

The instructor walked toward me, and I turned my head to face him.

"You're definitely a woman, and I can see how

much you want to be a pilot," he said, lowering my bra strap to expose my tattoo. He slowly moved behind me, walking away from the cameraman, who was repositioning himself. The instructor undid my bra and helped it slide down my arms. It dropped on the floor with a light noise, but my own breathing was now getting louder, deeper. My heart started racing.

"It's also a men's world, that's for sure," the instructor said as he hiked up my skirt. Then, he placed his hands on my hips and thrust his pelvis forward, pushing his erect member between my legs, poking my warm, wet panties. "I'll personally stand behind you and make all your dreams come true," he said. His dick twitched, and I couldn't prevent cock-hungry moans from leaving my lips. He bent me forward, pushing my body into a fold, letting my breasts hang loose. "You can do it in a men's world, and we'll do it together," he said, thrusting his erect member back and forth, rubbing it against my underwear.

"Cut! Wonderful!" the director said, bringing me back to reality. The instructor let go of me and walked away. I lowered my skirt to its normal height, then picked up my clothing from the floor.

After putting on my bra, I walked back to my seat, shirt in hand.

"Whoa, girl! What happened to the shy, reserved girl I used to know? I never thought you'd be comfortable doing that! What happened to you?"

I buttoned my shirt, trying to think of a way to answer my friend's question when the hot director stood up and addressed us again.

"Good job girls. The four of you who are still here have done a fantastic job in this audition so far. We only have one more scenario to go through with you before we elect the lucky one who will be representing Capt. Dick Harding Flying School for their next publicity campaign. We're talking about television, printed brochures, the whole works... and it pays well! This could be your stepping stone to a great acting career."

Katrina looked at me, her eyes spilling with optimism and unfulfilled dreams, her smile larger than ever. "One in four!"

Seriously? Katrina's this naive?

"Let's take a short break and meet again in the lunch room in fifteen," the director said before exiting the room.

"NOW, for the last part of the interview, we'll take you to a simulator. Obviously, we couldn't bring the real one here, but we've got a fairly large device in a private room and we'll have to do this last part of the interview individually so we can finally select the best candidate to represent the school."

The casting director pointed at Katrina.

"We'll start with you." He turned to the rest of us before continuing. "Please return to the waiting room in the mean time. Someone will come and get you."

I watched Katrina go past a door, then I headed back as instructed.

Using the key that was still wrapped around my

wrist, I retrieved my purse, then took a seat and read a few pages of an e-book on my phone.

Two chapters later, Katrina's voice broke the spell my crime thriller had put me under. I looked up. Her cheeks were blushed, her hair a little jumbled.

"Your turn," she said, pointing her hand toward the hallway.

I wanted to ask how it went, but she interrupted me before I even began. "Don't make them wait!"

I placed my phone back in my purse and handed it to her before making my way to the private room I'd seen Katrina disappear into thirty minutes ago.

4:15 P.M.

I KNOCKED and let myself in. After pushing the door open midway, my eyes couldn't help but focus on the large red plane sitting in the middle of the small room, surrounded by bright lights and reflective screens. The plane was reminiscent of one of those kid rides in shopping malls, but adult-sized and mounted on a much higher pole. A small step-ladder had been placed next to it. *Am I supposed to climb on this thing now?*

I scanned the rest of the room. My crooked-nose crush was sitting in his director chair, and near him were two cameramen and the instructor, in a bathrobe this time. All of them appeared ready for recording this last part of my interview, whatever it entailed.

Why am I doing this again? I have no real desire to get the part, *since there is no* part *to be had anyway.* But my genitals certainly wanted a piece of that director.

"Are you ready?" he asked, flashing a big smile at me.

Now's my chance.

"Listen, could we chat for a second?"

He shrugged then nodded.

"In private?" I asked.

After frowning for half a second, he requested that his crew get out, including Creepy Guy, who had been hiding, standing in a dark corner of the room until now.

Once all of them had gone, I walked up to the cute blond director. He got up before I reached his chair.

"Listen, I know this isn't real," I said.

"What do you mean?"

I lifted my fingers to wrap the rest of my words in air quotes. "Your audition for the—"

"Come on, you're so close. Onc in four! All you have to do is ride that plane. It's actually a lot of fun, like a carnival ride."

Curiosity had the best of me. "Really?"

He pressed a button on the small remote he held and the thing started moving. It went up and down, slowly at first, in a wave-like motion. It tilted a little to the left, then to the right... Then the speed increased, along with the sound of hydraulics or whatever was powering the contraption. The now jerky motion clued me in as to what it really was: a disguised mechanical bull like those used in country bars to test out the patrons' bull-riding skills.

"All you have to do is ride it—naked—smile and say one line: "Join me at Capt. Dick Harding Flying School, where fun is part of every lesson.""

I could imagine what the recorded video would be like. *Nothing but bouncing breasts. How uncomfortable would it be?*

"Listen, if you want to see me fully naked, all you have to do is ask," I said, my eyes fixed on his as I slowly undid my shirt, then tossed it on the floor. I took a step forward to close the gap between us then looked down to his waist. I undid his belt; he let me. I could hear his breathing getting louder and I could feel its warmth on my right cheek. I undid the metal button then slid down his zipper, the familiar sound only serving to increase my horniness. I couldn't wait to see what he kept hidden in his trousers, underneath the now visible black underpants.

"Is that so?" he finally said, his finger lifting my chin and forcing me to look at him again. His eyes were calculating. "So you really won't ride the plane? You're so close to getting the part."

Unbelievable. He's sticking to his story, still?

"I'd rather let my friend Katrina get the part, but..." I traced a finger down his chest from his collarbone to his waist. "I'd be satisfied with you doing me instead. Right here, right now. What do you say?"

His hands reached behind my back and undid my bra.

Finally!

Moments later, after having disrobed each other fully, he bent down to the floor to reach into his pant pocket and retrieve a condom. His erect and soon-to-be-covered cock was at the ready, strangely showing a slight bent comparable with the crook in his nose.

His lips swallowed mine without much of a prelude, as though he shared the same urges I felt toward him. My hungry lust, fueled by a full-day of partial nudity and tacky porn lines, could have lit a forest on fire.

I don't recall how we made it to the wall, but I

clearly remember having my legs wrapped around his waist when he thrust his swollen cock into me. A loud groan escaped my lips as my insides parted to welcome his large cock.

"You're so fucking wet," he whispered between two grunts. "And tight... Holy shit..."

Squeezed between him and the wall behind me, my back couldn't arch the way I wanted it to, but it didn't matter. I dug my finger in his tanned, hairless pecks. He was looking down, between my tits, staring at his own cock coming in and out of me.

His breath smelled of onion and curry, but it didn't matter. All I could think of was how to maximize my pleasure. I was already so close to the edge.

I let go of him and attacked my clit with frenzy, allowing myself to reach an orgasm before it was too late. I could hear the cadence of his breathing and grunts change. He too was about to come. My other hand squeezed one of my nipples just as he gave me the final push, my pussy throbbing with pleasure.

WHEN I RETURNED to the waiting room a few minutes later, once again dressed, fully satisfied and most likely rosy-cheeked, I headed toward Katrina. She was chatting with the instructor, who was still wearing his bathrobe. Katrina whispered something in his ear, then got up and walked out with me.

As we were about to leave the room, the young woman who had welcomed us earlier in the day addressed us again.

"Ladies, thanks for your time. We'll contact the lucky one by phone at 9 a.m. tomorrow morning."

Katrina sent a hopeful smile my way before turning quickly to wave goodbye to the instructor, who winked at her.

STARING at myself in the airport bathroom mirror, dressed in my real flight attendant's uniform, I couldn't help but mentally review what my relaxed getaway weekend had turned into.

Katrina and I never got a call—no surprise there. Lesson learned in getting screwed—both literally and figuratively—by manipulative, cunning... and good-looking men from L.A.

I was unsure if Katrina'd gotten any wiser from it...

Deep down, I knew she'd find success in this industry one way or another. Next time I'd see her could be on the big screen... or online porn. She had the body for it. I wouldn't judge her for making money using the talents given to her at birth... and those added by that skilled plastic surgeon.

Yeah, this past weekend had definitely offered entertainment in ways I hadn't imagined it would.

PART TWO

MY XXX EXPERIENCE

THE PLAN

I GOTTA SAY that re-reading this particular entry always gets me hard. And she's into tall blond men? She'll love doing me when I finally find her! This time, she's at least left a few decent clues behind. I know she's not based out of L.A., which isn't the most useful bit of information, but it's a start. My options for tracking her down are as follows:

OPTION 1: Use Facebook to find an L.A. actress named Katrina.

If I find one of her friends on Facebook, I could then go through her list of friends to find her (although I still don't know what she looks like). Facebook's search functionality to 'Find a woman named Katrina who lives in Los Angeles' may work, but would entail hours—if not days—of research. And what if her friend goes by Kate, Katie, Kat or some other nickname on Facebook?

Likelihood of success: Close to nil.

OPTION 2: Go to Los Angeles and find the aviation school.

I've got a name, I've got a town. An Internet search didn't bring up anything, though. Probably not a real school, just a scam made up by the casting agency.

Likelihood of success: Low.

OPTION 3: Go to L.A. and find the casting director.

Once again, I don't have much to go on, but I do have a description of the blond director. Feet on the ground and a few questions to the right people may work.

Likelihood of success: Low to average.

. . .

City of Angels, here I come.

You know my mysterious stewardess's identity. Get ready to share that secret with me!

WHAT HAPPENED

SINCE I FLY to LAX fairly regularly, I looked at my upcoming schedule and booked myself a nice hotel room for three days and two nights at the next available opportunity.

Sunny weather, palm trees, and beautiful people welcomed my gaze the minute I exited the airport. Sun rays—albeit hindered by the layer of haze—warmed my exposed skin. I put on my sunglasses and soon realized I should get out of my pilot's uniform and put on something more comfortable so I could blend in a bit more with the crowd.

I drove down to my Santa Monica hotel in the convertible I'd rented. While waiting for a traffic light to change near my destination, I smiled at a gorgeous brunette standing on a street corner. She wore the tiniest bikini top, sexy torn-up jean shorts, and a pair of rollerblades. Her toned skin had been kissed by weeks (or months?) of sunshine. *How I'd like to have a lick and taste her sweet goodness* L.A. certainly had more than its fair share of sexy residents I'd like to get acquainted with.

But my luck may have ended there, right at that traffic light.

After checking in at my hotel and donning a pair of white cotton shorts and a light blue polo shirt, I headed into town to visit my first of several talent agencies. Finding the right casting director in L.A. was more difficult than finding a needle in the proverbial haystack, even though I thought I had a good metal detector to help me with my task. How many casting directors could meet the exact physical description I had? I doubted crooked noses had become a fashionable item among the list of plastic surgeons' offerings in the area.

I did my best.

My first two days were spent digging, calling, visiting. I met with casting directors, talent agents, actors... I talked with anyone and everyone who could have possibly known the devious, crooked-nosed casting director.

My evenings were spent planning my days, scanning the local newspapers and online bulletins for shady casting calls and re-reading my stewardess's journal for clues I might have missed.

But my L.A. trip finally got interesting when I least expected it.

Here's what happened on my last day in Los Angeles.

WITH LESS THAN twenty hours left in this town, I was nearly ready to give up. While meandering to my parked car after yet another fruitless chat with an agent, an airplane-themed diner captured my attention.

Should I have another look at today's classifieds? I needed something. Another possible lead... Caffeine and food would certainly not hurt either.

I crossed the road and pulled open the diner's glass door, triggering a chime. Despite the deep-fried fish aroma tinted with burnt coffee that instantly reached my nostrils, the restaurant seemed popular: most tables were occupied, but two spots were available at the counter. So I walked in and sat on one of the old-fashioned stainless-steel stools padded with scratched up red leather.

A short and chubby waitress with a fraying gray chignon and dark wrinkly bags under her eyes came to me, coffee in hand. She wore a stained white apron over a black uniform.

"Coffee? Menu?" she asked, as expressive as the pot she was holding.

"Yes to both," I replied, smiling at her, hoping for a hint of amiability. It was in vain.

She reached across the counter, then underneath it, before pulling up a one-page laminated menu, which she handed to me. She flipped the empty mug that rested upside down on my paper placemat and poured me a steaming cup of coffee, then walked away, leaving me alone to browse the diner's slim food offerings. Most of the items were deep-fried.

I looked to my left and saw the remains of a burger and fries on the next patron's plate. Their fries appeared to be home-made and crisp. It had been a while since I'd indulged. *Why not?*

I placed my order when the waitress came back. Then I pivoted on my stool, taking in the aviation-themed decorations that included an antique wooden propeller, a wing stripped of its skin and paneling, showing the exposed ribs and stringers, and a dozen old picture frames filled with black and white images of the Wright brothers, an Antonov biplane picture, and lots of warplane photographs. I left my stool for a minute to go and grab one of the newspapers resting on a ledge by the door.

I returned to my seat with the mangled paper. It took me a few seconds to find the classifieds section, which I scanned. It was the same ads I'd already looked at this morning. I'd already talked to those people today. Nothing I'd missed. *Damn it.*

The waitress arrived with my plate just as I folded the useless newspaper. I thanked the emotionless woman, but she ignored me, obviously not keen on getting a tip. The burger did look juicy though. I lifted the top bun to include the side pickle I'd been given and then pressed all of the juicy bits with both my hands as I raised it to my mouth. The first bite was as tasty as expected, leaving a trail of greasy liquid dripping down my chin. I was chewing and enjoying every morsel while I let my eyes settle on the wall in front of me, which was littered with over a hundred business cards. I took my second bite when I saw something that nearly made me choke. Among the cards that were displayed in exchange for a free slice of pie and the right to be contacted by the diner for future promotions (according to a large sign on the same board) was pinned an exposed breast with tattooed wings above it, just like the photo shots that my stewardess had described.

I called up my waitress, and she immediately refilled my cup of coffee, at first ignoring my question, but then I begged her to let me see one of the business cards.

"No can do."

I slid her a twenty-dollar bill and asked again.

"The tit?" she asked.

I nodded.

She walked behind the counter, put down her pot of coffee, and then let out a sigh. She reached up and unpinned the card I wanted from the board then handed it to me. "I need it back," she said, holding the card between us, her eyes threatening me with shrouded, thunderous anger.

I nodded some more, trying to appease her, and she finally let go of the card.

I brought it closer and beamed as I recognized the beautiful breast I'd seen in the Mexico group selfie the hot lesbians had taken. The erect nipple, the subtle shades of light burgundy coloring her areola before the lightly tanned fleshy breast. It was tear-shaped, the perfect breast. A perfect C-cup, indeed. I took a picture of both the front and back of the Capt. Jack Harding Flying School business card and handed it back to the waitress. She sighed again, shook her head, and pinned it back where it had been minutes before.

She's probably made more money from showing that card than from her tips.

I finished and paid for my meal while trying to plan my next move. I had a phone number (no address), but I was pretty sure it wasn't going to be of any use.

After leaving the diner, I dialed the L.A. number and waited, pacing the sidewalk. Seconds later, I got my answer: an automated phone greeting announced the number had been disconnected. *Big surprise there.*

But two things were for sure: 1- It could have been the casting director or any one of his employees, but someone with that casting crew had been around this part of town in person; and 2- The photos taken that day had been published.

Could the video footage have ended up on the porn market? I didn't know how the other three finalists had finished their private audition, but I wouldn't be surprised if actual fucking had taken place. Based on the stewardess's journal entries, they'd recorded enough tacky lines for the movie intro. The instructor had been present for the final bit, ready for action in a robe... Published video footage could very well exist!

I decided to investigate this neighborhood more thoroughly. Google maps activated on my phone, I looked at my current location then searched for the nearest porn store.

ABOUT FIFTEEN MINUTES LATER, I saw XXX in bright red neon above a tinted glass door. I opened the metal-bar protected door and walked into the shop.

The store was much larger than it looked from the street. Dozens of shelves were staggered at various heights on the walls, displaying dildos, whips, and other adult toys. Five clothing racks held various latex, leather, and old-fashioned lace outfits for men and women. On the right, three aisles of movie cases covered the entire depth of the store, and on the left stood a Goth-looking cashier with pearl-like skin and long ebony hair. She stood behind the counter, surrounded by locked glass enclosures that displayed higher priced items. She wore a black leather top with a built-in girdle that pushed her fleshy breasts up. She deserved a closer look.

I walked to the counter and inquired if they carried porn movies featuring flight attendants.

"If that's what you're into. Of course," she said, her bright, luscious red lips moving and making me fantasize about having them wrapped around my cock. She winked, then folded her body over the counter, granting me the best possible view of her pushed-up breasts. She then pointed to the shelves where I could find everything I needed. "End of second aisle."

I took my eyes away from her tits and smiled, thanking her. I then walked away toward the videos.

I stood in the section she'd indicated and examined the tape and DVD covers that lined the shelves. It seemed both options were mixed together. Themes were obviously more important to them than movie format. I tried to find a cover with the school logo or an image I'd recognize, but couldn't, so I resorted to reading the descriptions at the backs of the cases.

About five minutes later, I noticed another man slowly approaching my section. He wore a long trench coat and sunglasses. Was he one of those perverts who flashed people in public? Why else would he wear a trench coat in 85-degree weather, on a bright sunny day? I didn't want to stay long enough to find out, so I scooped out every one of the tapes and DVDs that were related to my needs and headed to the cashier.

I didn't recall having seen a VCR or DVD player in my hotel room, but the Goth-cashier was kind enough to offer VCR/DVD player rentals as well, which I gladly accepted and paid for. Necessary wires and all.

She placed the items in a large canvass bag— thankfully unbranded—then winked at me as she handed me my rented goods.

"Thanks and enjoy!" she said.

3:00 P.M.

CALL IT EXCITEMENT, anticipation, or whatever else, but once in my hotel room, after rushing to hook up the rented DVD player, I froze.

Is today the day I finally uncover her identity? Will I finally get to see her body and look at her face on video?

I lined up all of my rented cases on top of my bed. There were twelve of them: eight DVDs and four tapes. Although none of the covers seemed to have been produced by the Capt. Jack Harding Aviation School, it was worth a try. (Not that I ever needed a reason to watch porn, but it was nice to actually *have* one.)

So I came up with a plan: I'd start with the less likely videos (i.e., the more professional looking covers), then work my way to the shadiest/crappiest covers. Yes, I was potentially keeping the best—or the very worst—for last.

I got in a quick shower, donned the fluffy robe that the hotel had provided, and inserted the first DVD in the machine. After navigating my way through the menu, I pressed play, then turned down the volume before sitting on the edge of my bed, remote in hand.

I watched the first two on 4X speed, resisting the instinct to beat off. The bouncing images were exciting enough, but my mind hadn't yet seen anything close to what the stewardess had described in her journal. Sure, lots of beautiful tits, inviting pussies, tight asses, and luscious lips, but nothing close to the images I was looking for.

I continued working my way through the other DVDs, limiting myself to the first ten minutes of each video. I set aside one that featured a blonde with a tiny ass and humongous tits as my back-up plan. If the stewardess didn't turn up, I'd sure love to give her a mental go.

Ninety minutes later, my pile of DVDs was all checked: no lucky winner. I headed to the bathroom and splashed myself in the face with cold water. Doing so, I realized seeing all of those hungry pussies had somehow made me thirsty (horny's a given here, of course). I returned to the bedroom and called room service to ask for a couple of cold beers to be brought up to my room.

While waiting for my refreshments, I unhooked the DVD player and plugged in the VCR in its place. I decided to also ditch my initial plan. I picked up the worst tape cover. My patience definitely had limits, and I'd reached them. The words 'Welcome to the Aviation School' had been printed on a white sheet of paper in large, bold black letters, then slid into the transparent lining of the case cover. Could be promising... But no image and no description on the back. I opened the case to find a tape with a blank TDK label—the type that came with new VHS tapes, something I hadn't seen in decades. That certainly didn't bode well.

"Here's to nothing... probably some dude's home video," I said aloud while sliding the tape into the VCR slot. The mechanism swallowed it loudly just as a knock resonated on the door.

"Room service," a male voice said.

I opened the door and let him in with his serving tray. Along with the two bottles I'd ordered, he'd also brought bags of peanuts, chips, and chocolate, one of which I purchased as well. *Clever up-sell tactic.* Eager to return to my unknown tape, I tipped him and sent him on his way.

Door now closed and back in my private porn-viewing universe, I cracked open my first beer, took a couple of swigs, then sat at the end of my bed, VCR remote in one hand and my beer in the other. I pressed PLAY and heard the old gears do their thing. Then, a couple of seconds later, a logo popped on the black screen: the same that was on the business card I'd photographed a couple hours ago.

"Holy shit! This can't be! I'm the luckiest bastard on Earth!"

Someone banged on the wall next door. I shut up but kept gloating on the inside. I took another swallow of my beer to celebrate.

As the Capt. Dick Harding Flying School logo faded, long legs in high heels took over the screen. Twenty or so women were lined up; the cameraman had captured their profiles, very slowly working its way upward, going from high-heels and calves, to thighs, and now bringing hot pink skirts into view. After showing the profiles of busty women in white blouses, the camera focused on the first woman, finally showing a face along with her torso: a tall, thin blonde girl with her hair tied in a ponytail smiled at the camera, hands on hips, her nipples poking through a shirt that was clearly two-sizes too small.

"Come on, come on. Show me the other girls. My naughty stewardess is on TV tonight!" I whispered to myself, feeling my cock grow. I rested my beer on the nearest flat surface, untied my robe, grabbed my shaft in my hand, and began thrusting into my open palm while watching the movie.

Transitions were unprofessional at best. Next, I saw a pair of long legs wheeling a suitcase. Then, another long pair of legs going up to a redhead in a Captain's jacket. Another crappy transition, then the shot moved to a panoramic view of several women, all tall and long-legged, seen from behind. Blondes, brunettes, red heads were within the group. Skin shades varied from very white to ebony black, probably a few Hispanic or Asian women in the lot. I couldn't tell which of the brunettes was my stewardess, but I remained hopeful I'd see her tits and would be able to place a face on her soon enough. Then, a snarling sound followed by a clipping noise echoed from the VCR. The TV screen flashed and froze on a distorted, twisted image of the line-up.

"Noooo!" I screamed.

Someone once again pounded on the wall. I shut up.

"Fuck, fuck, fuck!" I mumbled to myself.

I jumped from the bed and rushed to the machine. I pressed the EJECT button. Nothing. I pressed STOP, REWIND, POWER. Nothing.

I unplugged the damn VCR, then plugged it back in again. Each time the device emitted a mechanical gurgling sound, as though it was trying to spit out the tape, but to no avail.

The fucking VCR didn't just eat my only link to the stewardess. That can't fucking be! I have to break it open.

I looked around, trying to find a screwdriver-shaped object I could use to prop open the VCR and retrieve what was left of the tape. But then, smoke started oozing out of the slot, accompanied by a strong burned plastic smell, and, seconds later, the loud ringing sound of the fire alarm went off in my room.

Shit.

AFTER GETTING DRESSED and dealing with very unhappy hotel staff (thankfully, I stopped the events from escalating before the fire department arrived), I tossed my rented videos and equipment in the canvas bag and returned to the store, ready to give them hell.

When I arrived, the hot Goth cashier no longer worked the counter. She'd been replaced by a skinny little thing with blonde hair, half of it shaved, the other side tied up in a side braid, the tip of which rested on her barely covered breasts. Large blue eyes and a big smile decorated her face. Our eyes met, then she walked around the counter.

I headed toward her. I couldn't help but notice

her long legs half-covered with black diagonal nylons. The rest of her toned body was covered by two stretchy pieces of yellow fabric: one that barely hid her tits and the other, about the same size, that barely concealed her ass. Her flat stomach and metal-pierced navel were exposed. After taking a few more steps toward her, I was willing to bet she also had a ring through her left nipple, or one heck of a mole that was poking through the fabric of her top. There was no way I could be upset at that woman, especially since she wasn't the one who'd rented me the faulty VCR, so I let my built-up anger evaporate.

"Hi, I'm here to return the videos I rented earlier today, along with a faulty VCR," I said, placing my bag on the counter, letting the stench of burnt plastic fill the void between us.

"That's too bad. Did it swallow one of the tapes?" she asked, walking back behind the counter.

"You could say that," I replied. "But I would like to get another copy of the tape it destroyed," I requested.

"Let's see," she said before entering a code in her computer, then comparing my pile of tapes and DVDs with what her screen read. "Welcome to the Aviation School?" she asked.

"Yes, that's the one," I said, nodding and letting a flicker of hope raise in my chest.

She smiled and punched in a few more key strokes. "You have a thing for flight attendants?" she asked with a wink.

"Maybe I do. I'm a pilot."

"Really? You're a pilot?" She grinned at me, then returned her attention to her screen. "No, sorry, this was a one-off."

"What? No copies on DVD either?"

She looked at the screen again before continuing. "No, only this VCR tape. We bought it from a private seller. That was the only copy."

"Do you have his contact information?"

She hit a few more keys and looked at a few more screens. "No. I'm sorry, we don't."

What now. To come so close and to leave empty-handed?

"Could you try to retrieve it from the VCR?" I asked her.

"Our technician can try, but..." she waved her hand in the air. "Based on this awful smell, I doubt there's anything usable left." She returned her attention to the screen. "It will be an extra $25 for the destroyed tape and $250 for the broken VCR."

"What? You gotta be kidding... I can buy a brand new DVD player for less than $50."

"I know..." She looked around the store then bent over the counter to whisper the rest. "Listen, I go on a break in five minutes. What do you say you pay off that debt in kind? Think you can get me off and fly me to cloud number nine, Mr. Pilot?"

After the quantity of porn I'd sped-watched during the afternoon without coming, my cock made the decision without consulting with my brain. I nodded and smiled.

"Meet me around back. Go through the alley. You'll see a back door, just around a large red-brick wall."

I left her with my rented goods and headed out.

Having come so close to seeing my mystery woman to then find out I was once again helpless made me crave a cigarette. I hadn't smoked in years. I walked across the street to a nearby convenience store to buy a pack and lighter, then headed down the alley. I saw the brick wall, went around, then saw the blonde cashier leaning against it, a lit cigarette in her mouth.

I realized it wasn't tobacco once I got within a few feet.

She offered a puff of her nearly-gone joint, but I turned her down.

"I don't have much time," she said as I came

within ear's reach. She flicked the crutch of her joint on the bare asphalt next to us. Without any other warning, she dug her fingers behind my belt buckle and pulled me closer to her. Her lips swallowed mine while her hands fumbled to undo my belt.

Talk about going right down to business.

I reached for her top and brought it down, letting her firm tits hang loose and exposing a small ring piercing on her left nipple. I gave them both a squeeze, feeling myself harden. Her hand had already dug down my pants, grabbing out my cock, pulling me in toward her. I let go of her tits and lifted her skirt. No panties. A green lantern greeted me. *Leave it to L.A. stylists to groom your bush with a super-hero logo.* I lifted her by the waist. She wrapped her legs around my back, and I pressed her against the brick wall. Seemingly out of nowhere, she pulled a condom, opened it, and unrolled it over my erect shaft. Within seconds, I was pounding her, watching her implants barely shake from my rhythmic thrusting. She was caressing her tits, pressing them one against the other, hypnotizing me in the process.

"Fuck me hard, Mr. Pilot," she said, now biting her lower lip. "Get me off!"

I spat on a couple of my fingers and brought them to her clit. I massaged it as I increased my cadence, pushing my cock into her harder, deeper.

"That's the spot," she said. What were you doing when you broke that VCR?" she asked.

"What?" *Why is she talking?* I looked up at her. A tease sparkled in her eyes.

"Tell me. What were you doing when the VCR swallowed your tape?"

Guess words turn her on.

"You know, pleasing myself," I said.

"No, you're a pervert. Tell me what you were doing with your hard cock while watching those stewardesses get naked?"

Oh, she wants me to be graphic? I can play that game.

"I was looking at her pussy, wanting to lick it, but all I could do was grab my cock and give myself a good beating."

"Oh, you were a bad boy. You deserve a good beating." She unwrapped her legs from around me and pushed me off, making my dick come out of her. "Show me how you beat yourself off," she ordered, her own hand getting busy with her clit, her other still playing with her exposed breasts.

I obeyed, gliding my hand up and down my

shaft, the other tickling my balls. "Do you like it?" I asked.

"Yeah, I want to suck it. I want to lick your hard cock. I want you to beat yourself off in my mouth."

She knelt in front of me and pulled the condom off my cock. She stuck her tongue out, exposing yet another piercing. I moved my hand closer to the base of my shaft and dipped myself into her mouth. She closed her full lips around my cock, then reached for my balls, squeezing them together with her palm while the tip of her fingers caressed my anus. She brought her head forward, taking half of my cock into it. I felt it pound against the back of her mouth. She pulled back a little, then came back in. Faster and faster, her other hand pinching her nipples, pulling on her piercing.

A few garbled moans came out of her mouth in between swallows and licks. It was clear this wasn't her first blow job. I could feel myself close to the brink.

"I'm gonna come," I said.

"I want to swallow. Come in my mouth," she ordered.

I obeyed, and she locked her mascaraed eyes with mine. I came, pulled out, and the last drip of come fell onto her chin. She wiped it with a finger, then licked it off.

Then, just as if nothing had happened, she lifted her top back up, and pulled down her skirt. I tucked my cock back into my pants and did up my belt. That's when I noticed the security camera above the door.

I lifted my chin toward it. "Is this all on camera?"

"Of course, but don't worry. This is solely for the owner's private collection. She's a bit of a voyeur, and it's a way for customers to pay off certain debts. It's a win-win, really, right?"

"You do this often?"

"Not so much lately, fewer and fewer tapes get caught in VCRs these days, but we also have a 'service fee' for those who want to return or exchange a defective sex toy. You could buy one and try to return it tomorrow," she said, smirking, her hand tingling my cock through the fabric of my shorts. "Amelia's working tomorrow. She's hot. Listen, I'll ask the technician to recover whatever tape may still be in there, but I highly doubt he'll get anything out."

Based on the noise and amount of smoke that

had come out of it hours earlier, I shared her opinion.

A part of me was curious as to what hot Amelia could do to me in the alley tomorrow, but a larger part of me needed to get back to work. I had a flight to catch in a few hours. I also needed to plan my next excursion to find my stewardess.

NEXT STEPS

I NEVER HEARD BACK from the L.A. porn shop lady.

No doubt the sex tape from Capt. Dick Harding Flying School got destroyed.

Damn it, I was so close to seeing her face, but no cigar. I did toss that pack of cigarettes I'd bought in a moment of weakness the second I left L.A., and I'm proud to report it was still sealed.

At least I discovered how tall my mystery woman was, relatively. *I love long legs. Legs are my weakness (but come to think of it, so are asses... and tits...). I guess every part of a woman's body does the trick for me.*

I'm a weak man, what can I say?

You won't believe what my stewardess got up to

next. She's managed to find a very, very special castle in Ireland. An "all-inclusive" resort. They offer every service you could dream of, and everything is included. *Everything.*

Best part?

I know the castle's name and I've made a reservation.

Now, I just have to find a very open-minded lady to accompany me as I try and track down any clues left by my mystery stewardess in Ireland.

TO BE CONTINUED...

...IN PART 5 of *The Stewardess's Diary*, available at most major book retailers.

The complete episodic novel is also available in one (thick) paperback with exclusive author's notes about the series and what inspired each episode.

ABOUT THE AUTHOR

S.M. Pratt is a single woman traveling the world on her own, living in the moment, looking for more than love, and always trying out new things. Fun adventures and unique cultural experiences are always at the top of her agenda, no matter the country she happens to be visiting.

She would love to quit her day job and write full-time. You can help her write the next story faster by purchasing her books and/or giving her five-star reviews. Without your support, she's invisible and unable to make a living doing what she loves, which is creating what you love to read.

If you haven't done so already, please join her private reader group for previews, exclusive offers, and more. It's free: https://smpratt.com

For more information:
smpratt.com
info@smpratt.com